Keep Out Of The Dam, Sam

and other humorous stories for children aged 6 to 10

Sam and Annie Adventures

Written by Michael Faunce-Brown

*Dedicated to all those children, who enjoy reading my books.
May you have Good Luck and Good Health,
Determination and Respect for Others.*

CONTENTS

Chapter 1

Keep out of the Dam, Sam

Mum and Sam drove up to the homestead.

"This holiday is going to be amazing," said Sam excitedly.

Mum stopped the car in front of a big house. Turning to Sam, as she took off her seat belt, she said smiling at his excitement,

"This is going to be the best holiday ever!"

Annie jumped down the porch steps. She high- fived Sam. Mum carried their cases up the steps towards the front door. Sam's dog, Splash followed them from the car to the bottom of the steps.

"Splash, don`t do that," shouted Sam.

Too late! Splash had already started watering the bottom of the steps.

Toby opened the front door. He was a second too late to catch Splash but recognised the guilty look on Sam's face. He knew something was up but decided not to press Sam for an answer.

"Great to see you, Frances. Come on in."

"Leave Splash outside," said Mum.

Sam looked in through the middle of the house and out through the back window.

"Is that a lake?" asked Sam. He pointed out of the window.

"No, it`s a dam," said Toby. "Keep well away. We Australians call it a dam. It's a big pond for cattle and sheep to drink from.

"Why?" asked Sam. "I'm good at swimming, I'm in the school swimming team."

"It is very deep and dangerous. Keep well away. You can take Splash for a walk," said Toby, "I need to have a chat with your mum. "You can play with Annie. Not too loud."

"Great!" said Sam.

"Keep near the sheds and…"

"Don`t go near the dam," repeated Sam.

Sam and Splash walked down to the woolshed. There were hundreds of sheep waiting outside in a large pen for their turn to be shorn.

Splash ran towards the sheep. One jumped over a broken rail, escaping from the pen.

"Stop," shouted Sam as he chased after the naughty dog.

Splash stopped so quickly, Sam tumbled over him. He slid in the dirt and scraped his knee.

"Ow!" said Sam, rubbing his knee. Splash licked his face to say sorry. Laughing, Sam stood up and looked around for the sheep.

"Look what you have done!"

The sheep had already run half way down the hill to the dam.

"Silly dog, we better catch it before to makes it to the dam, otherwise we'll both be in trouble!"

Splash lay down, putting his paws over his eyes.

Sam was worried the sheep would drown if it fell in the dam. Could sheep swim? He ran towards the dam but Splash was faster and got there before him. The sheep took one look at the dog and leapt into the water. Sam didn't stop to think; he jumped after the sheep swimming, smoothly out across the water.

He was a good swimmer but had not stopped to remove his clothing and soon it was becoming harder and harder to swim because of the weight of the wet clothes.

Splash ran along the shore of the dam. Sam was still swimming well until suddenly he felt something tugging at his leg. It was a long tendril of pond weed.

"Help!" Sam tried to shout but instead he swallowed a mouthful of water. It sounded like more of a cough mixed with a gurgle as he choked on the words.

As his head bobbed above the water once more, he caught sight of the sheep scrambling out of the far bank of the dam, shaking the water out of its fleece. Splash did not know what to do.

He knew his master was in trouble but did he go back to the house and get the boy's mum or swim out to Sam. What should he do?

Splash looked first at the boy and then at the house.

"Help!" shouted Sam, clearer this time.

The weed wrapped itself round his other ankle and his head disappeared under the surface of the water for a couple of seconds longer this time. Splash sprang into the dam. He was swimming as fast as he could towards Sam. Sam`s yells grew weaker. Splash barked as he swam closer. He was worried that he wouldn't make it in time.

In the homestead Mum and Toby heard the bark.
"That was Splash!" said Mum. It didn't sound like it came from the barn, it was too far away. They both looked at each other, worried expressions on their faces; as

one they dashed to the door.

By now Splash was beside Sam. Sam reached out and rested an arm on Splash's back using the dog to hold his head about the water. As he floated there coughing up a lung full of water, he reached down and removed the weeds from around his ankles.

Weak and shaking from the shock of nearly drowning, he leant back and rested his head across Splash's back. Splash turned and took a mouthful of Sam's shirt and started towing him back to shore.

As they neared the edge of the dam Toby and Mum arrived still running fast. From where they were on the bank all they could see was a lifeless body being towed back to the shore by the dog. Toby leaped into the water swimming out to meet them. Mum followed but was just behind him. She hadn't been quite as fast, running from the house to the dam as Toby but she soon caught up with him in the water as she was a very strong swimmer.

Together they pulled Sam into the shallows and manhandled him onto the bank thinking him unconscious. He sat up and they stared at him in shock only now realising that he was okay.

Toby shouted at him: "I told you to keep away from the dam. What were you thinking?"

"I thought the sheep would drown," said Sam. " I'm sorry. It was my fault it escaped; it was scared of the dog and ran away."

Mum hugged him hard and close, shaking as she cried with relief.

They stayed like that for a while before returning to the house. Splash shook the water out of his coat just as the sheep had done a few minutes before and then lay down by his feet. Splash noticed that one of Sam's trainers was missing, taken by the dam never to be seen again.

Chapter 2

Ventilated Pants

Annie and Sam were in their favourite spot, the verandah.

"Sam, Mum says we can go to the creek and take a picnic," said Annie.
"Great," said Sam. "Go for a swim, after."
"No! Swim first," said Mum from the kitchen. "It`s dangerous to swim after a meal," she continued, "for an hour, anyway."

Sam and Annie set off for the creek. Each carried a tucker bag (like a lunch box) with food and water bottles.

They stripped to their pants and splashed out into the shallow water. Sam was carefully looking for weed. Luckily there was not any.

Puffed out they dried themselves. Dressed again they sat under a gum tree.

Sam suddenly jumped up. "It`s hot! I`m on fire!"

He dashed to the creek and sat in it.

Annie could not stop giggling. "Ventilated pants!" she called. "Someone must have not damped down their fire properly."

"I`d like to meet him," said Sam.

He squeezed most of the water out of his shorts.

"Are you hurt?" asked Annie.

"No, but my shorts are." There was a little hole burnt through.

As they were finishing their picnic, Sam sniffed.

"Do you smell what I smell?" he asked, jumping to his feet.

"Smoke!" yelled Annie, jumping up.

They picked up their bags and towels and ran.

As they reached the homestead Toby was pulling out a hose. Mum jumped out of the ute. "I was just coming to get you," she said. "Come and help."

"What do we do?" asked Sam.

"I`ll shut the windows and doors," said Annie.

"Spray the grass and shrubs, Sam."

A cloud of smoke was rushing towards them. Red flames glowed under it. Terrified sheep and cattle ran in front. Toby lit the grass just beyond where he had sprayed.

"He`s making a fire break," explained Mum.

Sam sprayed the walls of the house. They were soon running with water. Soon all the grass was burning. Toby let it burn. Then he sprayed the blackened roots. Mum let the dogs loose and barking hard, they helped Annie quickly divert the sheep into the yards.

"Spray them now, Sam," said Mum.

Annie soon had another hose spraying the woolshed. The smoke made their eyes sting. Mum tied wet handkerchiefs over their faces. She had cut tiny eye holes.

Toby handed round dark glasses. "Should help a little," he said.

Soon they could feel the heat. The wet wall of the woolshed was steaming.

"Get inside the shed," said Toby. He quickly tied hoses to the yard posts. There was a stream of water running down the whole wall.

Everyone was coughing but the wet handkerchiefs helped them to breath.

"Look!" said Annie.

Where Dad had burnt the fire break, the bush fire stopped. The sheep were bleating, panicked by the fire. They were tightly packed in the woolshed and under it.

"Well done, Annie," said her dad. "Some may die in the yards but you have saved over a thousand."

Annie said nothing but she felt proud.

"And you have helped save the buildings, Sam," said Mum. "Pretty cool!"

Sam looked pleased as he pulled off his handkerchief.

"How did it start?" asked Annie.

"Probably the same people as those who burnt my shorts," said Sam.

"He`s got air conditioned shorts," joked Annie.

They all laughed.

Chapter 3

An Accident

There was a beautiful sunset. Mum joined Sam and Annie on the verandah to watch it.

"Dad should be back by now," said Mum. She looked worried.

"Had we better go and look for him?" asked Annie.

"He might be anywhere in the west paddock," replied Mum.

"We had better be prepared for a night out." She hurried inside.

Sam and Annie helped carry out sleeping bags, water containers and food to the 4 X 4.

Dad was in trouble. His quad bike had overturned as it hit soft sand. Dad`s leg felt as if it were broken. He had pulled himself out from under a wheel and was sitting waiting for help. Tonight was going to be cold.

Mum, Annie and Sam were driving along a dirt track. Their lights lit up a kangaroo. It sat in the middle of the track as if daring them to run it over.

"Stupid creature," said Sam.

"The light confuses them," said Mum.

Mum sounded the horn. The kangaroo hopped off into the darkness. Mum drove on.

"I am worried about your Dad," she said to Annie. "We`ll stop here and listen. He might see our lights."

They stopped and got out of the vehicle.
"Gosh, it`s quiet," said Sam.
"Sh," said Mum. "Listen!"
Annie held her breath. There was no sound except for Sam`s breathing.
"Toby!" Mum shouted. There was no reply.
"We had better drive on," said Mum.
They got back inside. Mum started the engine. The wheels spun.

"Oh dear, we`re bogged down," she said, sounding tearful. "All out."

Mum dug away the sand in front of the wheels. She got in and tried driving out again. The wheels just spun round.

"We are well and truly bushed," said Sam helpfully.

"I`ve got an idea," said Annie. "Have we a wire strainer?"

"Yes," said Mum doubtfully. "We always carry one and spare wire in case of a broken fence."

"See that strainer post over there," said Annie. The headlights just picked it up some fifty metres in front of them.

"Clever girl," said Mum. "I see what you mean."

She pulled out the strainer and Sam heaved the wire roll out of the back.

Together they carried the wire to the fence strainer post. Mum tied one end of the wire round the post. Then she cut off a piece to tie to the wire strainer. Sam uncoiled enough to reach the vehicle. Mum tied the other end to the towing loop.

"Do you think you can drive this, Sam?" asked Mum.

"Yes," he said. "I have watched Dad."

"I will tighten the strainer first. Then you put her in low gear, four wheel drive."

"Yes," said Sam, "and drive very slowly. Dad has shown me how."

Sam got into the vehicle and waited till Mum had tightened the wire.

"Keep behind the car in case the wire breaks, Annie," said Mum.

Annie ran behind.

"Now Sam," said Mum.

Sam started the engine. He put it into gear. He let in the clutch very gently. Mum tightened the wire strainer as fast as she could.

Slowly the car edged itself onto firm soil. Sam stopped the engine.

"Excellent," said Mum, as they drove off.

"Where would I be without you two!"

"Up the creek," laughed Sam.

Suddenly they found Toby. He was shivering but so glad to see them. Mum carefully bound his leg to a broken piece of fence batten to keep it from moving. Then he hopped into the car with Mum supporting him.

"Like a kangaroo," he managed to joke.

Mum drove slowly to avoid hitting kangaroos.

"We don`t want any more adventures tonight," she smiled, as she told Dad about Annie`s brilliant idea.

Early next morning a small plane landed to take Dad to hospital.

"I know I am leaving you in good hands," he joked to Mum, winking at Sam and Annie.

Chapter 4

Paint and a Crocodile

Mum, Annie and Sam were sitting in the shade of the verandah.

"This old verandah needs a coat of paint," said Mum.

"Sure does," said Sam, pulling off a curl of blistered paint.

"We could paint it for you," said Annie.

"That is very kind of you, Annie but first it all has to be rubbed down."

"We could do that," said Sam.

Two hours later he wished he had not offered as he sand-papered off the old paint.

Two days later Sam and Annie were starting to paint. Sam mounted the steps.

"Be careful," said Annie. "The steps look wobbly."

"I`ll be right," said Sam as he balanced the brush on top of the paint tin.

Annie went on with her painting.

Sam was stretching off the top of the steps. He should have moved them first.

Suddenly he slipped.

"Aah!" he cried as he slid down the steps.

"Are you OK?" asked Annie, laughing.

Sam was sitting on the floor. He was covered with paint from head to toe.

"What do you think!" he spluttered.

"You look like a clown!" grinned Annie.

Mum came out and fell about laughing.

"I`m glad you think it is funny," spluttered Sam crossly.

"You had better get into the trough and wash it off," said Mum.

Sam jumped into the trough as he was. He sat in the trough while Mum scrubbed him with a brush. Annie howled with laughter until Mum told her to clean up the paint.

"Sam made the mess. He should clean it up," she moaned.

When Dad drove in from repairing fences, he was not pleased.

"That is $50 dollars worth of paint you have cost me!" he said.

"You had better help Annie clean it up."

As Sam and Annie were washing the floor clean, an indigenous boy walked by.

"Would you help us?" asked Sam, winking at Annie.

"Yes if you like," said the boy.

"What`s your name?" asked Annie.

"Charlie," said Charlie with a smile.

The three of them soon finished the job.

"Here, take this," said Sam, five dollars in his hand.

"She`s right" said Charlie. "I only did it to help you."

Charlie walked away into the bush.

"Now you have insulted him," said Annie.

"I thought it was the right thing to do," said Sam.

"Let`s follow him."

They ran after Charlie. As they ran, he ran. They came into a clearing. There were beautiful gum trees. They were reflected in a billabong.

Charlie dived into the billabong. He swam to the other side.

Suddenly a log like shape was chasing him.
"It`s a crocodile," shouted Annie.
"I must stop it," said Sam.

He ran to the far side of the billabong. Charlie was dragging himself out of the water. He was tired after his swim. The crocodile was only two metres behind him.
Sam picked up a sharp gum tree branch. He stood beside Charlie as the crocodile

snapped at his ankles. Sam drove the branch towards the crocodile`s eyes. It stopped and blinked. The branch just missed his eye.

Charlie jumped up. Annie threw stones at the crocodile. It decided it was not that hungry. It turned and slid back into the water.

"Hey thanks," said Charlie.
"I guess we are heroes," said Annie.
"I only did it to help you," said Sam, smiling. He felt pleased with what they had done.

Charlie smiled and vanished into the bush.

Sam and Annie skipped their way home.

Chapter 5

A Fantastic Ride

Sam and Annie were waiting for Toby to saddle the horses.

"Sam, I will give you Sleepy," Toby said, "since you have not ridden much."
He helped Sam to mount. Sleepy pranced around a little. Sam gripped his saddle tightly with his knees.

Annie mounted her horse, Lucky, easily.
"It`s Okay. He will settle down after a good gallop," Annie said. She walked Lucky to outside the yard. Sam followed feeling nervous.
"Not so fast," he called, as Annie trotted off.

Sleepy was not going to be left behind. Sam found he was jogging up and down uncomfortably. Lucky was cantering now. Sleepy copied. Sam found it was smoother. He started to enjoy the rush of wind in his face.
"Good, isn`t it," called Annie.
"Too right," agreed Sam, as he caught up.

Suddenly Lucky stumbled. Sam was flying through the air. He hit the ground hard. Everything went black.

A light appeared at the end of a tunnel. Sam was stumbling out of the tunnel.

A big rough man was whipping another. The man, who was being whipped, had chains round his ankles. Other men were breaking rocks with sledge hammers. All wore chains attached to heavy iron balls. Every man was bearded. Most were very thin. They all wore rags.

"I`ve gone back in time," thought Sam. "They must be convicts."

The overseer suddenly noticed Sam. "What are you doing here, boy?"

Sam froze. The overseer looked very frightening. He grabbed Sam.

"We`ve not got chains your size, sonny. I`ll tie your ankles. You won`t go far like that." He laughed cruelly.

Before he knew it, Sam was tied. He was only able to hobble a little at a time.

"Here, you can shovel the dirt over the edge. Don`t stop till I tell you," the overseer said.

Sam took the shovel and began to scoop the smaller stones over the edge of the road. The overseer left him. He picked up a bag. He pushed its contents between some huge boulders.

"Take cover," shouted the overseer.

The convicts stumbled away from the boulders. Sam did so too. The overseer lit a fuse.

It spluttered and hissed towards the boulders. There was a loud crack and a roar. Smoke billowed and pieces of rock flew everywhere. A convict pulled Sam down behind a boulder. It rained pieces of stone.

Then there was a cloud of dust.

"Thanks," said Sam. "Can`t you escape?"
The convict smiled and patted Sam`s shoulder. He did not say anything.
Suddenly Sam was pulled upright by the overseer holding his ear.
"Ow!" exclaimed Sam.
"You are giving him silly ideas," said the overseer.
"You can peel those potatoes and keep your trap shut."
He shoved Sam down beside a sack of potatoes and gave him a peeler. Sam looked shattered as he saw the size of the sack.

The nice convict crept up behind the overseer. He pushed the overseer over the edge of the road. Sam saw him tumbling head over heels.

"Hey! Thanks," said Sam.
"That`s O.K.," said Annie. "You are breathing again. Great!"
"What?" said Sam as he sat up. "I don`t feel too good."
"You were out for ages," said Annie. "I gave you the kiss of life."

She helped Sam to his feet. They walked their horses home.

"They`d never believe me," said Sam to himself, thinking of the convicts. He was covered in dust and his ear felt sore.

Chapter 6

Flying High!

Sam and Annie were out for a ride. It was hot and dusty. Both were thirsty.

"Let`s give the horses a drink at that billabong," said Annie.

"Yes, and we will have one too," agreed Sam.

They dismounted at the billabong. The horses drank thirstily from the clear water. Sam and Annie drank from their water bottles.

"Hey, that`s good," said Sam. Annie nodded, agreeing.

Sam mounted his horse, which suddenly pranced about nervously. It bolted with Annie`s horse close behind.

"Wait for me," shouted Annie as they disappeared in a cloud of dust. Annie heard a rumbling noise behind her. She turned and stood amazed.

A shiny round object was landing close to her. As she watched, mouth open, a door opened. A ramp slid to the ground. Annie stood rooted to the spot with wonder. A strange looking man with oval face and a shiny silvery suit descended the ramp.

He beckoned to Annie. She felt she had to discover what was inside. Annie walked towards the ramp. The man stood aside to let her past.

Suddenly she hesitated. "Is this a good idea?" she asked herself. Mum often said she shouldn't talk to strange men and this one was strange alright. The man saw her hesitate and pushed her up the ramp.

Annie tried to back down the ramp. The man blocked her way. Before she knew where she was, she found herself inside the shiny machine. She stopped again, looking in wonder at the men and women also in shiny space suits. Annie was guided forward by her captor.

For a moment he stopped and she looked back at the hatch. It was too late. The door was almost closed.

"What have I done?" she said to herself. The other people crowded round her. They touched her face, as if she were a strange object.

"You are the strange ones," she said.

They chattered in wonder at her words. There was a hush as a tall woman arrived wearing a long cloak.

"Let me go back to my family, please," said Annie.

The woman said nothing but gestured towards a door. Annie was gently propelled towards the door. Annie felt frightened. She wondered what was through the door. They entered what looked like a science laboratory. There were cylinders in one corner, and glass door cabinets with trays of instruments.

Annie was firmly propelled towards a couch. She suddenly found herself lying on the couch. She tried to struggle but they strapped her down. She could not move.

Rubber pads were attached to her forehead. The flying saucer was humming in flight. Annie felt a tingling in her head. "Are they finding out what is in my brain?" she wondered. She could not help grinning as she thought: "Not very much!"

Gradually Annie fell asleep.

Sam had reached home. His horse stood chewing grass, as if it had done nothing wrong. Mum came out looking worried.

"Where is Annie?" she asked.

"Back by the billabong," said Sam.

When Annie woke, she was lying by the billabong. There was no sign of the flying saucer. She felt slightly sick. There was a roar as Mum and Sam drove up in the 4 X 4.

"Hey, that was some ride," said Sam. "I nearly fell off several times."

Annie thought about telling them of her adventure.

"They`d never believe me," she thought. "Was it a dream?"

"How did you get those funny round marks?" asked Mum at bedtime.

"Can`t think," said Annie, smiling secretly.

Chapter 7

The Flood

Sam and Annie were sitting on the verandah. They were playing a new board game called "Tread Quietly". It was a battle between Smugglers and Coast Guards.

They were interested in the game, so they did not notice a big, black cloud. It swept across the sky. Suddenly heavy drops of rain rattled on the roof.

"Oh no!" exclaimed Annie. "Dad and Mum are in town."
"What`s wrong?" asked Sam. "They`ll be back soon."
"The track can be washed away," said Annie. "Last time the creek washed away a bridge."
"What about the sheep?" asked Sam. "Will they drown?"
"We had better open the gates to the woolshed," said Annie.
"Some can go inside and hundreds underneath."

They sprinted across to the shed.
"Drowned rats!" exclaimed Sam, as they squelched into the woolshed.

Crowds of sheep were following them inside.

"I`ll let the dogs in too," said Annie. She splashed across and released them.
The four dogs shook their coats dry. They only had oil drums to live in.

There was a floor board and just the gum trees above to keep them cool.
"What about the other sheep and cattle?" asked Sam.
"They will make for the high ground," said Annie.
"No worries! They don`t mind the wet. I just hope they get there in time."

Annie`s dad and Sam`s mum were in the ute. The windscreen wipers were on fast. They could not clear enough water to see through. Toby slowed down.

"We will have to stop," said Toby. He slowly drove onto higher ground. He stopped the engine.

"I hope the bridge will hold," said Jenny.

They could see the water rising. The creek below them became a raging torrent. Whole trees floated past. One struck the bridge.

Quickly the water rose over the bridge. There was a splintering noise.

"It`s going," said Toby. The bridge was swept away with a crash.

"We will have to drive back to town," said Toby.

"What about the children?" asked Jenny.

"They`ll manage," said Toby. "Annie knows to stay indoors."

"And the sheep?"

"We`ll lose some unless they can get up to the wool shed," said Toby. "I hope she has remembered the dogs."

Toby started the ute and turned it round.

"Lucky we have four wheel drive," said Jenny as the wheels spun. They slithered back along the track. Mud splattered everywhere.

In the woolshed Sam and Annie sat shivering in a pile of wool.

"Getting warmer," said Sam.

They could not get back to the house. A torrent of water flowed past.

Toby and Jenny drove slowly along the track to town. The water on the track was about twenty centimetres deep. When they reached safety, Toby tried to ring Annie again. There was no reply.

In the woolshed the sheep were quiet.

"I hope Mum and Dad are O.K." said Annie, worried.

"What if they drowned?"

"They won`t," said Sam quickly. He bottled up his own thoughts.

Their worries were soon over. A roar sounded outside. They rushed to the door.
Toby and Jenny waved to them from a jet boat.

Chapter 8

Annie`s Bunyip

Another school term had passed. On the cattle station it had not rained for ages. Toby, was very worried.

"If we don`t get any rain soon, I will have to sell most of our cattle and sheep."

"We must have some left for breeding," said Sam`s mum.

"My dad might let you leave some by his creek," said Sam, who was staying with them once more.

"A nice idea but he will want all the water he has or he will be as badly off as us," said Jenny. "Our vegetables are dying too. Do ask him Toby."

Next day Toby and Jenny drove off to Sam`s property.

Annie and Sam sat around on the verandah trying to keep cool. The sun was like an oven. Suddenly around the corner of the shed strolled a dark boy of about fourteen.

"Hi! I`m Bunyip!" he announced.

"Hi, I`m Sam," said Sam.

Annie said nothing but clutching Sam`s arm, ran indoors. She slammed the door behind her.

"What did you do that for?" asked Sam.

"A Bunyip! That`s a river monster!" said Annie. She was as white as flour.

"He`s no monster, you twit!" laughed Sam. "He`s an indigenous teen-ager."

There was a tapping on the door.

"Don`t answer it," whispered Annie.

Sam hesitated. Annie was making him nervous. Sam went to the door and opened it.

Bunyip was standing there. He too looked nervous.

"Have you some water, please?" he asked.

Annie suddenly became brave. She went to the tap and poured him a glass.

Bunyip stayed outside the door.

"Come in. I don`t bite!" laughed Annie. She could not be frightened of someone, who was frightened of her!

"Where are your parents?" asked Bunyip.
"They`ve gone to find water," said Annie.
"I can find ngama," said Bunyip, "if it is there."
"Bet you can`t," said Sam.

"Watch me," said Bunyip. He went outside and pulled a twig off a shrub. He held it out in front of him and started chanting.

Suddenly he started walking towards the house.
"It is in here," he said as he entered.
"Of course it is. It`s in the tap," laughed Sam.
"Not much left," said Annie.
They followed Bunyip into the house. He stopped inside Annie`s bedroom.

"Have you got a chamber pot? asked Sam, giggling.
"Course not," said Annie and she started to giggle.
Bunyip pointed to beneath her bed.

"Down there," he said.

Sam disappeared from the room.

"Well I guess water is more precious than floorboards," Annie said. "There`s a loose board where I hide my precious stuff."

She knelt down and pulled up the board. Below there was just earth and a cardboard box. Annie pulled out the box with care. She put it in her cupboard.

Sam entered with a trowel and bucket. Bunyip took the trowel and started digging. He quickly filled the bucket with earth. Sam staggered out with it to the flower bed.

Soon they noticed the earth was damp.

Suddenly a trickle of water began to fill the hole, already half a metre deep.
"Ngama," said Bunyip. "Water"
"Great!" said Sam. "You are a wonder."
"I`ll get a hose," said Annie.

"I`ll knock a little hole through the air brick," said Sam, and soon he had done so with a hammer and chisel.

They watched with pride as the water flowed out into the flower bed.

"I won`t be able to keep my precious stuff under there again," said Annie sadly. "What is more precious than water?" asked Sam.

It was only then that he noticed Bunyip had disappeared.

"Bunyip!"

"Wonder boy, not monster," laughed Annie.

"We had better think what to do with the rest of the water," said Sam.

As Toby and Jenny drove up to their home, they were full of joy.

"Sam's wonderful dad has allowed us a paddock by a creek to water our breeding stock," said Toby. "But what's all this!"

A flow of water trickled along little channels through the vegetables. Already they looked greener.

"Just Annie's Bunyip," joked Sam.

Chapter 9

Annie`s Robber

Annie and Toby got out of the ute. Sam followed them with his bag. He was staying with his neighbours once more.

"Something is wrong," said Toby.

The evening sky agreed. It was glaring red, orange and purple. The quad bike had gone. Toby hurried towards the shed. They followed him. Toby picked up a broken chain.

"Look! The blighters must have had a bolt cutter."

"Try to catch them?" asked Sam.

"Easier said than done," said Toby.

He looked angry. "I only bought it a month ago! What sort of people steal other people`s work tools!"

"Will you buy another quad bike?" asked Annie.

"I will have to. Horses are too slow for cattle and sheep mustering*."

"When do you muster them?" asked Sam as they walked towards the house.

"We round up cattle out of the Bush for the sales, and sheep for shearing," explained Toby.

They went in to see Annie`s mum.

"Hello Sam! You have grown in the last few weeks. You are tall for eight," she said, giving him a hug.

Sam enjoyed the smell of her clothes.

That night Sam and Annie shared her room. They were chatting as soon as her mum put out the light.

"Suppose the robber comes back?" asked Sam.

*N.B. "Mustering" is collecting together.

"We could catch him," said Annie, bravely. A shaft of moonlight lit up her face.

"How?" asked Sam. "He might be big and strong."

"Set a trap," said Annie.

"He might trap us," thought Sam. "What sort of trap?"

"You`ll see," said Annie.

Sam thought of a giant mouse trap and smiled before falling asleep.

Next day a truck pulled up outside the shed. Sam and Annie watched as a brand new quad bike was off loaded.

"Hey, Dad had better hide that one," said Annie.

Sam and Annie were looking around the shed for trap ideas.

"What about this?" asked Sam, pulling at a large net.

It was bundled up in a corner.

"Yes!" said Annie. "We could hang it up over the quad bike."

That night Annie woke Sam. "I heard something," she whispered.

They crept out to the shed.

"No one about," whispered Sam.

They crept into the shed. Annie shone her torch on the bike.

Sam got onto the quad bike and pretended to ride it.
"Get off. I`m going back to bed," said Annie.

As she turned the net fell over them and the quad bike.
"Got you," said the robber as he tightened the draw rope.
"Three for the price of one!"
He quickly reached through a hole in the net and stuck some tape over Annie`s mouth. Sam sat on the bike, too frightened to move. The robber approached him.

"Mmm..mmm.mm," said Annie.

Sam woke from his trance. As the man reached through a hole in the net, Sam switched on the bike. He started the engine with a roar. The robber tried to stick the tape over Sam`s mouth. Sam let out the clutch. The bike shot forward. The robber was tangled in the net.

The bike dragged Annie and the robber out of the shed.

Sam rode over to the house front door. He stopped the bike and revved its engine. The door opened. Dad came out with his rifle. He could not help laughing when he saw the robber tangled up.

When the police arrived, they praised Sam`s quick thinking.
"Well done, young man. We have been looking for this robber for months."
"My idea," said Annie.
"Yes, and look who it caught!" laughed her dad.

Chapter 10

Sam`s Snake

Toby, was cleaning out a shed.

"Hey, Annie! Come and look at this."

Toby held up a long, black musical instrument.

"It`s a clarinet," said Toby. "Like to try it out?"

"Yes please," said Annie.

Annie blew into it. There was no sound.

"You`ve got to wet the reed," said Sam. "A boy at school plays one."

Annie put it into the water tank.

"No, not like that," said Sam. He licked the reed.

"Disgusting!" exclaimed Annie.

Annie washed the clarinet mouthpiece in the water tank. She blew and a shrill sound came out.

"Disgusting!" said Sam, laughing.

"Keep practising," said Toby. "You can busk in town and make loads of money."
"Yes, selling ear plugs," laughed Sam.

Toby drove off to mend some fences.

Sam was reading under a tree. His book was about a boy and a girl, who were always getting into trouble. "A bit like us," said Sam to himself.

There was a rustle from under a bush.
"A lizard," thought Sam. He went on reading.
A long brown snake eased itself into the sunlight.
"Who is this in my garden?" thought the snake.
Sam read on, unaware of any danger.

Suddenly a shadow snaked across his page. Sam looked up. He froze. He knew that brown snakes are very dangerous. Once bitten, one has only four hours to get to hospital. This one reared up.

Annie was playing her clarinet on the verandah.
"Enough practice for one day," she thought.

The snake was swaying from side to side.

"How dare this human come into my garden," it thought. It was getting very angry.

Annie suddenly noticed the snake. She screamed. The snake reared up ready to strike. Sam`s face was white with fear.

Annie suddenly remembered a film of India and a snake charmer. Very slowly she inched her hand towards the clarinet.

The snake was quite still. Annie started to play soothing sounds. She swayed the clarinet from side to side. The snake began to sway from side to side.

Very slowly Sam moved away. When he was about three metres from the snake, he rose to his feet and walked backwards. As he reached the Porch, he jumped up the steps. The snake slithered away.

"Oh Annie," Sam gasped, "You play beautifully!"

Warning: Not all snakes like music! Not Heavy Metal!

Chapter 11

Fire Again

It had been hot for weeks. Sam and Annie lay in the shade of a tall gum tree. They had hollowed out of a bank of earth a tunnel over the weeks gone by. They shored up the sides with wood from old fertilizer pallets. They came out the other side. They found a rusty old water tank. They placed it on its side and pushed it hard against the tunnel, so it made a little room.

Then they covered the tank with the soil from the tunnel. Mum and Dad didn't mind. It kept them busy even if muddy.

They watched a possum asleep near the top of a tall gum tree.

"I bet it's the one that's stealing all our oranges," said Annie.
"We get enough to eat," said Sam, "you can't blame it...? What's that smell?"
"Smoke!" shouted Annie. "Mum!"
They ran inside where Mum was ironing."
"It's only this - a bit hot," said Mum.

She still looked out of the window and froze. A cloud of smoke was rolling towards the house, a kilometre away.

"Where's Dad?" asked Annie.

"Way over there, mending fences," said Mum, pointing in the opposite direction.

"I must warn him." She picked up her mobile phone.

"The battery's flat. Oh dear!"

"He'll see the smoke and come," said Sam.

"Not till too late. He's over the hill. Quick, we must wet the house." Mum rushed out of the house and snatched up a garden hose. She turned on the tap. Mum hosed down the weatherboard side nearest the fire.

Already they could feel the heat of the fire. Sam found another hose and started wetting down the garden. Annie just stood watching the fire. It was roaring towards them. She felt so helpless. It must burn the house and them too. What could she do? Suddenly she had a brainwave.

"Mum, come away now. It'll be here in five minutes. Come down our tunnel."

Mum turned and went pale as she saw the flames roaring like a beast towards them.

"You go down the tunnel. I'll be with you in a minute," she gasped. "I must just grab my purse and things." She disappeared into the house.

Sam and Annie ran to the tunnel entrance and waited for Mum. It seemed ages before she reappeared with her purse, some papers and a photo album.

"Quick! Get down there!" she gasped, beginning to choke from the smoke.

Sam disappeared down the tunnel like a rabbit. Annie followed him, hoping Mum would fit. Luckily they had made the tunnel quite wide, and she scrambled inside just as the roaring fire roasted the out buildings.

"Our poor house," said Annie. "Everything will be lost."

"But we're safe in here," said Mum, "Thanks to my two rabbits." She hugged them and laughed.

"What about Dad?" asked Sam.

"He's got the ute. He'll drive to the other side of the dam. He'll be okay," said Mum, secretly hoping she was right.

"Where will we live?" wailed Annie.

"We could always go and stay with our cousins on the coast," said Mum.

On the far side of the dam, Dad watched the blaze fizzle out as it reached the water.

He was so worried as he watched helplessly his house explode and could not stop his tears as he thought of his family, who could never have survived.

Eventually the ground was cool enough to drive to the house site, a twisted iron roof, a heap of smoking timbers and nothing else.

"Mum, Annie, Sam," Dad yelled, hopelessly, tears streaming down his face.

It was a such a shock when first Annie, then Sam then Mum eased out of the tunnel, coughing from smoke but all unhurt.

Dad just stood there and cried with relief. They had the longest hug-in in History.

THE END

If you enjoy these stories, you might like your parents to email me and I`ll write some more.

When you are twelve, you might like my "Tom In Trouble" £4.99 including p.p. and "The Vampire's Apprentice" £7.50 also including p.p They can be ordered by my email mrfbrown@hotmail.com

Mum and Dad might enjoy "Blowing My Own Trumpet", and "Tom Won't Break" available from Amazon and Waterstones..

Illustrated by Chantal Bourgonje
Advisor: Barbara Townsend

Michael Faunce-Brown

mrfbrown@hotmail.com Copyright 2017